Mostly Me

The Collected Works
(1969-1994)
of
James H. Buckingham

Published by Buckingham Publications
Crystal Lake, Illinois

First Edition

First Printing • 500 • June 1995

Library of Congress Card Number: 95-94254

ISBN 1-885591-80-2

Additional copies may be obtained by sending
a check or money order for $10.00 (includes postage)
to the address below. For your convenience, an order form can
be found at the back of this book.

Buckingham Publications
P.O. Box 602
Crystal Lake, IL 60039-0602

Mostly Me *may be obtained by retail outlets at special rates.*
Write to the above address for more information.

Printed in the USA by

*M*ORRIS
PUBLISHING

3212 E. Hwy 30
Kearney, NE 68847
800-650-7888

Contact Morris Publishing for a FREE
guide to publishing your own book.

Dedication

To my unborn children
Jesse James, Galena Sue and Katherine Anne
May you forgive me someday.
To all of my six children,
By Blood,
Anna Catherine, Emily Christine, William James,
and Elizabeth Caroline,
and by Marriage,
Tracy Renee and Matthew John.
It is for you and yours
that I write.
To my wife, Susan
whose smile and touch
brought the Cave Man
out of the Ice Age.
And gave me love,
untempered
by dominance and submission.
To my Mother,
who did the best
she could,
and stayed–
for the children,
May she rest in peace.
To my Father,
who did the best
he could,
and stayed–
and sacrificed himself
may he become
himself one day; and now
May he rest in peace.
To Grandma Sherman,
who provided
a safe harbor
during the storms
of childhood,
May she rest in peace.

To the City of Winnipeg and
The People of Canada
who spared me
from the Vietnam War,
may you always be
apart from
the United States,
and choose
FREEDOM
over economy.
To my ex-wife, Marieluise,
who never wanted
children,
and gave me
four.
To the parish of
Sts. Peter and Paul,
who were there
waiting,
when I came home
again.
To my brothers
And sisters,
May they all
find peace,
in their own time.
To my readers,
May I share
my sorrow
and joy.
And to God,
From Whom
All my writing
flows.

CONTENTS

Part 1
Stories to Say

Part II
Songs to Sing

Travel Song

As in life, as in travel,
it's not where you're going,
it's not where you end up;
the journey's the thing.

Caution!

Freeze-Dried

(Just Add Tears)

~ Part I ~

Stories To Say

1

Passing

My car was still in repair so I had to walk. I started my walk at 9 in the morning and by the time it was noon I was in the country. I walked down the one road that led to my destination. I went by the farmhouses that were interspersed along the road by their respective cornfields and pastures. The sounds were of farm machinery harvesting, an occasional car going by, and the sound of my feet disturbing the gravel on the road. Every farm along that road seemed to have a dog, sometimes two, one for barking and one for biting. Some mothers would call their children into the house, other children would gather together in a group for better protection as they saw me coming. The biting dog would be held back so I could walk on by unmolested, but the dog was still kept in ready till my figure was quite farther on down the road. This was all done because I was not known, an unknown, whose dress and manners were city; I was the city intruding into the country and I was a dangerous animal to be watched out of the corner of the eye till I was away where I could do no harm. I might be able to disrupt the quiet order of country life, and because of this, I became a dread.

At my sight, the cows, bulls, horses, sheep and hogs gave me all their attention. They were used to the cars that sped by but were really not used to me, being that I did not speed by, but walked, I could be seen. I was unfamiliar and, "Just what the hell are you doing here anyhow?"; I fancied the animal's query to be. The horses and sheep would all be as one head, I first attracting their attention, then like one, they turned their heads to follow my movement past them until I was no longer an interest. The bulls sometimes would go and spread the news and gather for a conference over what was to be done about me. The hogs would charge the fences, and the cows looked comical when they would break into a trot with their heavy haunches swinging up and down in a rocker motion as they came for a closer see. But it did not matter, for I was going to see my love.

By the time I had traveled the twenty miles from my city to her town it was 4 o'clock. My feet hurt and I had four water blisters on my toes, for my shoes were not meant for hiking, but I knew that my walk had a purpose. She was surprised to see me, for my intentions I had kept a secret. She was wonderful as always. We went for a stroll, did some shopping, and just sat and talked, glad to be with each other. There never seemed to be any time, for when I had thought it but a while ago when I first kissed her that day on meeting her at the door, it was now night and time to go to bed. I was tired and so at first slept with my love aside me. Later, after a bit of resting, we engaged in that act of consummation that drew us together into one, the wish to totally fuse with another's love forever. And then lying on our sides, facing each other, sometimes kissing, I thought of how wonderful this was, only some other thoughts started coming in too.

The different thoughts were out of place and I wished them away, yet they remained. These were the moments beautiful but still those renegade suggestions said something opposite. These were transitory moments, they would fade, would not last long. A feeling started inhabiting me that I did not want. And then tears came and I cried. With every additional tear my supposed manliness was wept away. I cried as a small child alone in the middle of an open field crying over the loss of something, crying for all the universe to hear and crying all the more because the child knew that the universe did not care to listen. And my love asked me why I wept, over what had I all of a sudden become unhappy? I found that it would be hard to explain, I really did not know if I could make myself understood to her, if I could understand it myself. Maybe she felt it too, for some of her tears fell onto my cheek, or was it that she did not wish to see me weeping? Things seemed so cruel during my grief.

Because it was all this - - what could I have said? - - that I would have to go away again by the morrow not to return till next week. Because it was away with each step that I would have to go. I would once more have to travel down that rural road, that gauntlet of suspicion. Although it was not the physical parting that affected me so much, but the memory. Love which is ever so tangible, those moments, would not last; the memory would sink back in my mind and each time make it harder to recall. Details would be gone and occurrences could only somehow be remembered by their significance. Everything sank on down that back road of time, where there was no stopping, and life passed by you and me as a memory, where it faded and was erased out by other memories; until, there was no memory of us in anyone.

Fall 1969

2

Plight

Laughter from in and out of the cell that holds the hollow, the pit abscess, to the cheek that chortles the product gasped within the vocals vocalizing all these poor utterances:

See if I can leave, Oh! that I could have left it behind on the tumor of my backbone in underbrush the midpoint vertebrae. For going is not go, either concrete congregate or flower flaying festival still here near; travel far topaz of the eye's minded but mine own no nevertheless lacking avail. And they say I am free, Free! Whooo! do I coo, what unnecessaries of lies to fore me unto thinking it. Just all where solid can I move? Can I pass free, brother? Do I need these many margins line and hieroglyphic cuneiform to go here and yon from my block to block to visit the bars making inner blockin'. And I can't breathe, can't move plus hearing no more heaving talk but tapes and said words told saying. But for on I am told in being tolled by being.

Being costs --- taxes, meters, registers, stores, tickets, charities, "Your donation all, would be appreciated, and we appreciate so much, you just will not be pressed, to come in, unless; you share with us." ------We like beatifying you do too you must retort. Snort, snort, snort to sniffle again my own without being taxed on trying to check past the guard of the hairs, the stuffed nose, or the stuffing of me and the people celebrating the god holiday pie, we let loose, ere a day only necessity returning earning paper green to live to give all, back or break it. The heat say burn whose water tends to help the scorch but buy your ultraviolet free or harnessed.

All only to laugh more the more every matter condensed energy, well energy, just that, owning different varying tunes vibrations but man oh man ah child but for woman that bad vibos vibras make entirely utterness going down foraging for, my vibration rhythmics ascending horror. Hey old and new, had and has, together assembled had what a sheer horrible is all the vibrations, lukewarm unfeeling leukemia; my laughter fills the Cries, the 'ole crying for the filling of the jar that only empties echo. Shrieking askance, my messenger intrepider, flying rescuer, again back to mine ears as my same uncanny giggle crying, masks the mind to save on. My own making is that just returning for nor are any returns coming. Alone to die! Sprung and stretched oblivious, hilarious laughing trapped universe making made perchance a thousand to infinity by thee bad vibration. A very, very bad one combination, emanating existence.

1969

3

Homo stupidus, man the stupid

A well-to-do man was relaxing in his study, sitting comfortably in his plump leather chair by the fireplace. He was reading about the latest manned moon landings. A dog was also in the study and was clawing at the closed door so it could get out and be where there were no sly, little games save the natural game of survival. Things would be fine in this snug world of artifacts with all its trickeries unless a sudden something went wrong.

"Hey! Who turned the lights out?"

The man fell on the floor, his chair and magazine disappeared. There was no fire anymore. Everything was black.

"What the? Damn! It's getting cold!

"Where's my dog? Where's Fido? Where are you faithful Fido?"

"Where am I? I can't see a thing. Everything's completely dark."

"What the hell is going on here?"

"Whatever this is, I think it a sick joke."

The man started moving about to get out of the room that was no longer, to go open the door to light and warmth which wasn't there. He bumped into something that he could not confront, there seemed no way around it. Then his arms became useless, falling down loose at the sides, all voluntary use was gone. A vague thing jostled him from behind. And before he could speak, physical blows began to fall on his body.

"What is happening?"

"Stop! You wouldn't beat a man who can't defend himself!"

"I can't use my arms! Why me? What did I do?"

Harm still came to him and the hits went to his face now. All remained dark and his fear heightened. He tried to kick his invisible attackers away from him, thrashing all around while his arms flapped from side to side. It was all to no good though for he was overpowered and was kicked and shoved to a certain place.

The dead dark had the sounds of an operation, the man was just being finished up on.

"There. That is the end of the suture."

"Nurse, do throw those glasses of his away."

"Yes doctor."

"Say that was some operation though."

"Yes, it was quite a job removing all that fat of his."

"His belly's much the slimmer now."

"I wonder if he'll be able to make it?"

"Fancy, it's almost like a test for us all."

"Doctor. Doctor."

"Huh? Oh, sorry. Thinking to myself."

"What is it that you want?"

"Doctor, what am I to do with his clothing?"

"Here, let me feel them."

"My my, what fine cloth he did have."

"Suede leather and velvet."

"Too bad he doesn't have any fur himself."

"Get rid of them, they can't do him any good at this stage."

"Nothing can help when he's left to his own nakedness, to his true, bare self."

The man woke up in a forest that was bright with the day. He was naked and his body was without bruises. The fat on his stomach was gone and his health was good. His nearsighted eyes tried vainly without his glasses to see what it was that was coming towards him across a clearing. Two hunters in deep red jackets with scopeless, high-powered rifles were closing in.

"Look, look, if that isn't one of the dumbest animals over there, it hasn't even moved yet."

"I don't remember seeing anything like that before."

"Let's move in a little closer."

"Wait, it's finally noticed us."

"Balls, a lame deer can run faster than that."

"Here let me shoot it. It's running so slow, it's an easy shot."

"All right. Go ahead."

The slow animal was an easy target and the hunter downed it with the first shot. The two hunters walked across the clearing to see what they had.

"Wait a minute, look what it is."

"Damn! I shot a man."

"The bottom of his feet are all cut up, feet aren't any good for running. A hoof or paw is much better."

"What do we do with it?"

"Shit, I don't know. It isn't worth a thing. Let it rot. It won't last long."

The two hunters went back to their campsite and slept the night in their sleeping bags. If you were there again at the campsite the next day, you would see two bears. Now bears are sloppy eaters and bits of red polyester cloth were in their mouths. Overnight one of the most severest cold fronts to ever hit that part of the country came unpredicted. Some cloth was in the bear's mouth and some of the hunter's still frozen flesh was lying in the bear's stomachs.

A dog was sniffing around in the woods, it glanced over at the rotting corpse of the man, and then faithful Fido went on to go hunt for a rabbit or two.

1969

4

"The Caterpillar in the Practical and The Butterfly in the Pure"

I

Alone figure searched the nearby rocky foothills in search of himself. The heavy, pensive man was going down, down, down went he to town; the town cried to swallow him for five days more. Spruce, fir and the pine go by -- Thomas leaves the needles to their wind and chill. Looking back he sees his former intrusions in the snow, climb up and into beyond, through the brush and the aloof trees on the fringe, till finally dark holds true court and unquestioned authority where the footprints can be seen no more. And as he turned, himself cried out, "Do not forget me next weekend, I will be here - waiting." The two cries pulled on each other, one from the mountains, and one from the town, and found good battle in Thomas' mind.

He found the road's end and followed it backwards down. The town stood out as a missing segment in the mirror, a hole in the center, all else was a soft shine of old reflections, used light; the stars admired themselves in the glass on top of the snow. Drawing nearer and nearer from above, the town below appeared to slowly grow like a spreading, thinning liquid. With sight came sound and the faintly discernible hum developed with each down into the normal noise of the town. Even an anthill on its own scale is a hubbub.

The fair size town of Representiyou lay like a fungus on the foothills not too distant from the range of the Rockies, so thought Thomas as he stepped on Representiyou's streets.

How I love these mountains! I was born here in Representiyou but I'll be damned if I want to die here! This town's very existence and others like it threaten the wildlife, soon all the woods will be pushed into only little parks within the ever expanding cities, and then they'll be gone too. Since a child I remember looking down on Representiyou from the mountain slopes and wondering how people could do this, there it was, the town, a stain in the green that surrounded it, gnawing at the green sides of its borders like a team of cold, clipping caterpillars. But how could one fight himself when everyone in the whole town fed off of one another as a total organism. There was a web that held the people together: people needed food, houses, clothing, gas, oil, fixtures, furniture, hardware, medicines, mail, electricity, appliances, games, government, diversions, protection, service maintenance for the animate and the inanimate, and a multitude of other things in which a person can get an occupation in at the expense of others. Specialization, everyone needs everyone, supply-and-demand, the national economy, the standard of living; living? We are all ants, feeling thought only for the moment when we are stopped in our task to be done or yet to do, in fetching the food, fighting the enemy, or courting the queen. The mounds sprout up and raise the earth, and when their number becomes too many they will deathly char and annihilate all the ants to a peace of particle precipitation. Killed by their pride, ignorance, sense of security and mushrooms.

Thomas now approached the street that led up to the apartment building where he lived and was a janitor to pay for half his rent. Thomas only got half his rent free for his services because he was but a part-time janitor. He did what work there was to be done at night since the building was rather new with all the modern conveniences, that sufficed. If there was some urgent matter to attend to during the day the owner came himself, this situation seldom occurred. In the day Thomas worked at the grocery store that he half-owned with Lloyd, whose father before him half-owned the store with Thomas' father. Thomas' parents now no longer exist.

Thomas noticed a card taped on his mailbox as he entered the building. It was a note from Mr. Mire who lived next door. On Thomas' mailbox above his name was the word, "Engineer". The word engineer adds more dignity to a janitor's work in a like manner as the word executioner does to a killer. The card read:

> I have dropped a spare key to my apartment in your mailbox.
> Use this key to open my apartment to fix the leaking toilet.
> When through, lock my door and drop the key in my mailbox.
>
> Mr. Mire

Thomas took the key out of his mailbox and went up the stairs to get his tools.

Mr. Mire's one bedroom apartment was an example of his proper and practical character. His apartment was always in a perfectly ordered condition. No thing frilly or of a decorative nature would be found in Mr. Mire's place. Mr. Mire worked as an accountant from four in the afternoon to midnight. His life was a ledger balanced.

Thomas fixed Mr. Mire's toilet as best he could, at least nothing should go wrong with it for a while yet to come. The problem was of a bad seal on the joint that connected the pipe of the water main to the pipe leading to the back of the toilet. Little puddles were on the floor because of the leak. Water usually finds its way through connections, making leaks, drips and burst pipes a continual problem of plumbing.

After finishing work and putting the key in the mailbox of Mr. Mire, Thomas ate and went up to the roof. Here on the roof again, to be on the roof at night gazing at the mountains. Thomas searched with his eyes during his five days of imprisonment on a certain area in the mountains. Every night in his five day sentence for years he tried himself. Now in his heavy coat fortified against the stratagems of winter, Thomas would stay up here until sleep teased his favor and he would go down to bed.

For Thomas a secret concerning his own nature, his being, his life, lay somewhere in the mountains. Even now, glaring out of his invisible five day bars, he pined for his meaning which he knew was in the wilderness and not in civilization. From early childhood Thomas felt a natural draw towards the mountains for their beauty, serenity, their stateliness, but his life with the mountains took on added dimension after a particular event while he still was a senior in high school. Sitting on the roof, Thomas being 15 years older, supported himself by his five days of work -- his prison. On weekends he searched for that riddle, that other mystic Thomas identical with himself. The years of his fruitless weekend searching was dividing his person over what he should do. He realized that he could not modify his life much longer by confining himself in Representiyou for five days while he was being shredded to nothing during that time. But Thomas was not a man of ample means, he did have to sustain himself. The thoughts hammered his head excruciating, incurable torment, and though the falling snow obscured the mountains entirely from his seeing anything clearly, he saw everything. The whole sight, clear as always it came back to him, the whole memory vividly discerned once more.

II

Calm. There is an attitude of calm in falling snow even when the wind and the sky forces it down faster and faster and harder into one's face. I can't really see the sky though, I shouldn't have come up this time. What a foolhardy person I am turning into, thinking I am above the weather! If I get out of this one I'll be more to the cautious from now on. Of course I may say it now, but I will most likely do the same thing later. But Thomas let's stick to the present and cope with that. I'm too far above the tree line to make it back and I have to find shelter, for a blizzard has no manners. I must move quickly, the dark is painting more black every time and if I am caught in the open as cold, snow and blackness increase, this is the last mountain trek for Thomas. Up along the mountain wall in the rocks I might be able to find some shelter, I have to try.

This damn snow! I'm freezing! My fingers are numb, at least my feet still hurt. I can't see where the hell I'm going!

Thomas trips over a large stone and falls flat in the snow.

I'm so tired and cold! I can't give up. Crawl! I'll crawl. I have to keep moving, I must find shelter to get out of this. I can hardly control my body! The snow is endless. I'm losing control of my arms! I have to rest a little, my head feels so heavy. . .

Fatigued from exhaustion, losing consciousness, he drops his head hitting a rock under the snow. The pain arouses Thomas to a dim sensibility. Reacting to the pain and the warm blood falling over his face from his cut forehead, he tries to rise on his feet, unable to assist with his hands, he flounders and falls over, tumbling through a snow bank into a small recess in the rock. The accumulating snow during the storm forms an overhang along the ridge on top of the sheer wall of the mountain causing finally with its tremendous weight, an avalanche. A great wall of snow lunges down the mountain side in a rolling, rocking wave that laughs at the tall and portly ponderosa pines with a smite that levels the huge feathered poles to the ground, buried in white; and the same mighty behavior is done on down the slope until the wave hits its rocks and becomes a breaker, its energy expent and the snow is leveled off with its victims. The snow wave filled the opening of the recess that Thomas had fallen into, sheltering him from the wind and the cold making his cave insulated and heated from the warmth of his body. The avalanche had also sealed him in under 15 feet of snow. He would die if unaided.

The cut he received on his forehead was not deep and was already coagulating while he lay sleeping in his capsule. The danger of gangrene had passed, for once given a chance to warm, his body responded and blood was circulating. With having had some rest and feeling returning to his limbs, Thomas came back into the life of the human aware and shook off the first shivers. He was quite weak.

Oh, my head! I.., blood?! I guess I'm lucky not to have hurt it more than this. Still have to get out of here, I'm cold and hungry, but I think I can do it. First lemme warm up these toes of mine, oooh! my fingers are frostbitten, the burn of countless pinpricks. Nuts, I'll just start burrowing out of this fallen snow here - I'll just...

When he started to try and dig out of the snow, to his surprise the snow only fell in, starting to fill up the rest of the recess. After minutes of experience he understood that he was buried.

So I sit here and wait to die? My but that isn't that refreshing. How will anyone know I am underneath the snow when they are looking for me on the top? This is absurd, I'm dead. Now if I can convince myself...

Thomas went on in this way, pretending with himself, but still hoping for rescue so he would not have to die. The hours were taking the time punctually, the fatigue of his body had almost carved away the last of his power to remain awake when he heard the soft sound of snow being moved. A grin was moving across the pallid face of Thomas. The sound from above drew closer, he could hear hands scraping the snow. Light was coming in from the world which he considered he would not see another time. There was but a human to come in and break him from the capsule, a saviour.

But the saviour came and the saviour expected did not coincide. A man, yes it was a man, crawled into Thomas' cavity. He was covered with long, thick hair on his body that had deep, coarse skin. The hair covered his entire body except for the areas around his eyes and nostrils. The man, the thing, must have had a light with him for now everything was bright. The man moved towards Thomas. Too weak to move or cry out, Thomas noticed that it had no mouth! No opening at all where the mouth should have been, only skin across the face! And the light that made everything bright was from something glowing in his forehead! The man approached nearer yet and the word stood out, the pulsating glow of blue-white letters etched in his skin; the word, "PURE"! Thomas became unconscious, half from extreme fear and half from weariness when the man touched Thomas' rotund belly.

One sees with eyelids closed a crimson red light when facing the sun. The blizzard was done, the sun shone hot to bake all the fresh quantity of snow it had recently received. If snow was black it would be melted within the hour and the sun's rays could reach the ground and heat crusty earth till we all felt the warm, and it would be summer in midwinter. Thomas lying out in the open on the melting snow blinked in deference to the sun. The ball of yellow brilliance awoke him.

Thomas was in the state that lies between the two worlds of conscious-ness and unconsciousness, a stuporous daze. His stomach pained him and felt so strange! Things were gone, a time to let by the will to live, a time to sleep, for once and all...

III

Sleep was a nagger, it never gave up, besides Thomas had to go to work this morning; so he descended from the roof and went to bed.

Sitting in bed he mused and wondered how much luck a person could have. A search party had found him lying on the ground and took him home for his mother to take care of. And how she fussed! Thomas was in bad shape, but he still could feed himself. Through it all he kept his secret that he discovered on waking up before he got home. No one ever saw. And the writing in the snow he did see, the mouthless man saved him -- resurrecting him from the tomb, he was real. The writing by his saviour in the snow was clearly written and he knew that in the two sentences was the secret, the words went: "You must be me before you can be me. I am you!". His memory was clear, the words stuck fast, it was real. Lying in bed he slowly moved his fingertips over the word that the mouthless man had given him on his now thin stomach, he felt out the letters one by one, the coal, black carving of the word "PRACTICAL" across his stomach; that was all too real.

The next morning saw a bright day in Representiyou. Thomas' night overshadowed the day, he had not slept well, he was disturbed. He walked the few blocks from his apartment to his half-store, not a supermarket but a neighborhood grocery store that did good business. Lloyd had already opened the store, Thomas was late.

Lloyd had always thought of Thomas as did most everybody, that he was a little screwy. A real weekend mountain man. It was bad enough that he about died from exposure in the mountains when he was young, but he relentlessly kept going to them. Not since he was in high school had anyone seen him go swimming. Most people associate Thomas with his arrest of 5 years ago, charged with assault and battery and disturbing the peace at his parents' wake (Thomas parents' wanted to die together so neither would get lonely when the other died, so they committed suicide together -- togetherness) for punching a relative in the jaw because he was gossiping and laughing too loud. Thomas was ok though. Lloyd's relation to him was that of an acquaintance like most everyone else.

Thomas had come home from work at the store and was sitting in the kitchen. He sat filled with anxiety ever aware of the burnt carvings in his stomach, he was falling apart. On the kitchen table was a letter from his younger sister Jane, it was an open invitation for him to come visit her. Jane, now Mrs. Jane Idol, had been married a short time ago in New York. Thomas didn't go to the wedding because New York really was too far to go. Jane and her husband moved to the West in a city not far from Representiyou. Maybe a change of place? Why not, he thought. A vacation was due him as a janitor, a call would take care of that. Still, there was the store ---

"Lloyd?"

"Yes, Lloyd here. Who's this?"

"Thomas."

"Thomas who?"

"Thomas at the store."

"Oh you. Yeah, what do ya want, hmmm?"

"Could you manage the store alone a week?"

"Obviously, But you have to be back Monday, there's a new year coming up you know."

"Yes I know. I'll be back in time. Thanks."

"Don't worry you are going to do the same for me."

"Click."

"Click."

Thomas had yet to call the Greyhound Bus station to see what time the next bus would leave. The matter of never meeting his brother-in-law did not affect him, he was searching for an escape and making a visit to his sister's was a possible way.

"Greyhound lines are temporarily busy, please hold on, an operator will take your call. Do not hang up! Greyhound lines are temporarily busy, please hold on, an operator will take your call. Do not hang up! Greyhound lines are temporarily busy, please hold on, an operator will take your call. Do not hang up! Greyhound lines are temporarily..."

"Click."

Thomas packed a small suitcase and went down to the bus station where he decided he would rather wait than not hang up. The snow was falling, the mountains were in the background.

There was approximately a mile to go, according to directions, Jane's house was straight up this road. On the way there one thing entertained me, four poles of traffic lights. It was at night but the time said it was a new day. But how much time will man and machine get? I could not help thinking who was the dumber of the two, man or machine, seeing those four separate sticks with their alternating lollipop colors of red, yellow and green. They were too big for toys and all they seemed to do was blink at each other and blush in shame, for they went on and off throughout the night with no one to heed them. And I did not consider them, I did not stop, but walked right through their intersection and dared them to stop me with their silly colors.

Thomas' sister groggily welcomed Thomas at 3 a.m. when he came to her house. She had him go to sleep in the guest room and then she went back to bed. The next day Thomas met his brother-in-law and his sister-in-law, who Jane introduced to Thomas as, "Your single, pretty sister-in-law, Susan Idol". Thomas enjoyed the rest of his stay and then returned to his town.

Thomas started spending his weekends in Jane's, or say, Susan's city. The mountains were forgotten. Over the months Thomas grew fatter than he had been in his chubby youth. The word "PRACTICAL" expanded on his stomach like an inflated balloon. He discovered he was acquiring friends, people liked him, that he was beginning to be like everyone else. Seven months after their introduction Susan and Thomas were married in the city. Although the wedding and the reception were small, by the time that Susan and Thomas arrived at Thomas' apartment in Representi-you the effect of the day's festivities had wearied the couple.

IV

It is wedding night. Thomas is washing his hands. Susan, his fresh 24 year old and young bride is waiting for him in bed, nude. The rustle of sheets can be heard.

Hell, I'm so damn tired, I don't feel like doing anything tonight. I'm just tired, that's all, tired. A person needs sleep.

"Thomas, are you coming to bed?"

"Sure Susan. I'm coming."

Thomas came out of the bathroom wearing an old, fading bathrobe. He did not take off his bathrobe until he was under the covers in bed, so that the cuts on his fat stomach would not show. Thomas laid his bathrobe on the floor and turned the light by the bed out. The room was quiet and uneasy. Susan, after a few minutes spoke.

"Well?"

"Well what?"

"This happens to be my wedding night!"

"Strange, it's mine too!"

"A funny thing, I married a man who doesn't love me!"

"I do. I'm just tired."

"Tired!"

"Look, is love a fuck? Sex isn't love."

"True, but it's a natural part..."

"Then allow me a little sleep, ok"

"All right."

"Good night Susan."

"Good night Thomas."

Needed rest is taken by the two. The sun is up. Thomas feels warm from within and without. An extra amount of heat is derived from each source. The body of Susan is alongside Thomas' own. Susan is awake and arousing him. He turns around to face her and embrace her. There is an air full of expectancy in her eyes. Sexual play is preparing for the union. Susan rolls over on her back, Thomas shifts into position. A sheet is lifted. One could see clearly in the room, Thomas sees Susan's body full-length.

Motion froze. There she was, eyes closed, yearning to have her great, gaping wound widened, cut, bled and fulfilled! And there it was too. Across her stomach and across the lowest part of her abdomen, the ashen word! And in horror Thomas looked down at his own body seeing that it was not only on his stomach but now on his sexual organ! The tar word of "PRACTICAL"!

A shriek was heard in the apartment that had the sound of extreme terror and a sense of a deep moan somehow. A shrieking, hairy man ran down the stairs where his cry was muffled. Mr. Mire stood at his door in his bathrobe intending to find out the cause of this loud disturbance. The former Miss Susan Idol, appearing in the hall from her apartment, ran nude with her legs spread wide not after Thomas but quickly to Mr. Mire next door. She flicked on his "PRACTICAL" and went into his room, bed and him, so she could be sound and secure before she would think of her dying an old maid virgin another second.

Mr. Mire's seal broke, the water was flooding.

V

A mild July day could be seen approaching. The sun's direct rays fell upon all. The dew felt a haste to go down into the earth. A day, today, for swimming in the summer would be. The youth, the town (for today was Sunday), had risen early. A call to the water would bring many and most to the town's new and large civic pool. In anticipation, swimsuits were donned and a number of people walked to the pool.

The quiet morning was interrupted by shouts and screams originating from certain streets. A wild, hairy man with no mouth and the blue-white word of "PURE" in his forehead was running down the streets. While some ran away, others promptly prostrated themselves as this dread went by.

Thomas had come to a sudden understanding in the bedroom when he saw the word not solely on himself, but on Susan too. The strange saying of the mouthless man had become clear and Thomas started merging with his being. By the time he reached the bottom stairs in the apartment building his mouth was gone and in the street he became the mouthless man. He ran, running with fear. And his speed increased when he saw the "PRACTICAL" marks on the bodies of the people in their swimsuits as they were walking in the streets. Thomas kept on his fleeing course, running upwards towards the sanctuary of the mountains.

VI

The wind is blowing and sweeping all of my hair to one side. Up on this crag there is not too much that I cannot see of the town. The earth has a life of its own, it erupts, falls, splits and spins. The life on this planet more than coexists with the world, it depends on it, and I am sure that the earth could spin on very well without it. Man was not invited to this planet. He depends on the earth and others, he has a certain quality of halfness about him, an incompleteness. He has built an ant system where interaction is impersonal, dependency a must and a sense of responsibility that derives from positive and negative reinforcement. There is no living in an anthill. One cannot take much time out of reflective thinking unless there is a filled tummy, an eased state of mind, an absence of pain, the germ to do the thinking and the time to do it in. Need necessitates practicality. And then there is my case.

I have metamorphosed farther than merely a caterpillar to a butterfly. I am the butterfly in pure essence. I need neither nourishment nor sleep, I am naturally protected, am independent in myself. I am not tied to nature, can be a nonparticipating observer. All my thoughts are abstract. I have been saved, resurrected. I understand the words: "You must be me before you can be me. I am you!". I had to follow his steps before I could be one with my saviour. I had to realize, to be aware, to reject the practical before I could merge with his being. By some chance I was chosen, resurrected, and now I stand up here above; one with my resurrector. I am secure.

But what of the pure? What of the blue-white star, the brightest, must it pulse and expand and contract forever? Is there an order that balances, a prime mover? There is no basis to support a yes or a no. Yet the practicals do not regard the star at all, for they must be practical.

I image I could discontinue my thinking for I see something. The town has to alleviate its fear. I can see a hunting party moving up the mountain from the town that is representing you, armed with their silver swords, charms and bibles to come and kill the fear physically. But then I am quite an implausible character. I am safe. For I, Thomas O. Jesus, am not real. ARE YOU?

1969

5

On Drafting a Pardon

When you sit amongst yourselves around a table reviewing my application I feel that without this letter you may never have an inkling of what the bumpkin can be, so let me relate the past years as they tangent with the draft.

On August twenty-eighth, nineteen hundred and sixty-eight I registered with the local draft board. This was something every male at age eighteen had to do yet this posed no immediacy as I had saved my money from earnings as a construction laborer that summer and was going to Northern Illinois University in DeKalb, Illinois for which I would get a college deferment. Now I didn't go to school that fall just to keep from being drafted, I wanted to go, but then in growing up with Vietnam it was nice that certain things went hand-in-hand.

Dormitory life in a thirteen story high-rise did not suit me and as this was a requirement for freshman I withdrew from Northern and moved to the Chicago YMCA from whence I stayed with a friend I met at NIU for a week at his parent's house in Wilmette till we found our apartment in Chicago. I had lost my II-S deferment since leaving DeKalb and in the meanwhile applied at the University of Illinois at Chicago Circle. I attended the spring and summer quarters full-time there and worked nights at the Main Post Office throwing around mailbags to support myself. By August I quit the post office as I could not sufficiently study for the postal clerk's zip code and route tests while still going to college. I left the big city and its dirt for good and went to live with my parents in September, enrolling at Rock Valley College in Rockford.

Since I had not completed a full thirty semester hours within one year, I was reclassified I-A. In December of '69 I was ordered for my pre-induction physical. I asked our family doctor if he would write a brief letter stating the truth that I had a condition of bronchitis since early childhood (around age 3) and that because of such would become severely winded from strenuous exercise, especially running. My doctor refused as he said, "It wouldn't do you any good anyway." I am no respiratory cripple to date (my mother and one of my sisters have asthma) and on the average get an attack about once a year but have me run 200 yards and I am too pooped to pop with inflated lungs -- puffing to get the air out. In 8th and 9th grade football running practice I ended up last, far behind the biggest tubbies (I'm of medium build) and the farther we ran the further I wheezed back. I was depressed during the physical thinking I had come to cattle-call instead of an examination and did not bother with their test. We were told it's impossible to flunk. I was recalled for another chest x-ray and the doctor asked me how long I had bronchitis; and I passed.

I took a routine school physical to return to Northern in January 1970 through my doctor. My chest x-ray showed up abnormal for which I had a fluoroscopy at a hospital, the results being benign pleural adhesions of the lower lobe in the right lung. In order to finance another year of schooling I took out a $1,360.00 loan through the Illinois Guaranteed Loan Program. By becoming a full-time student again I was granted a IS-C deferment allowing 1 year to catch up in the required number of semester hours lacking.

By early 1971 I was I-A as I had not caught up to schedule and back to brass tacks and facts. I applied for a conscientious objector status so that I might do alternative service as I would never be in an army or such, believing that one must always be responsible for one's own actions and when one is under circumstances of taking orders one is not in control. I hold too there is no such matter as temporary loss of control and accordingly never have nor will get drunk or high and reduce this total consciousness. The letter I wrote to them then still holds sway in my regard and attitudes; this being voted down 4-0 by the board with no reason given. I always waited the full time in appealing and filing matters for the maximum delay but thwarted myself this time by getting the dates confused and therefore I appealed my CO vote a couple of days late whereupon I received a letter replying my appeal was past the time limit, there is no extension, and report for induction June 21 (approximate date, the details of memory blur with age). I was outraged and mad and forthwith sent them a nasty postcard, the one thing that burned my bridge, a stupid and immature act but I can't waffle on its writer, written to people he never met deciding his fate.

I had other avenues. I had broken my right leg in a motorcycle accident on April 21st that year, for which I was in the DeKalb Public Hospital for two days (no cast), missing two weeks of work. In June it was still sore and had a slight limp, this would have put them off for awhile. Or such as one friend I knew got dental braces and a temporary deferral. I needed braces but didn't have the money (P.S. I have them on now, they're a pain in the ol' keyster). The bag of tricks was not gone, I became a melancholy magician. My life was becoming procrastination incarnate, I had resolved against such involuntary servitude and if no one would believe my reasons -- be damned.

I continued working in DeKalb to October when I left the country to take up residence in Winnipeg, Manitoba Canada procuring a job and landed immigrant status in December 1971. Leaving a place where one is raised with the thought that one might not be able to come back is hard. It is more than the idea of sneaking a forbidden cookie out of the jar, family, girlfriend, the home milieu. I never assimilated North of 49 because I never tried to. The new Americans were by and large deserters with whom I could not identify, all quickly melting into the culture even to purposefully picking up the speech differences and English spelling. My orient was South.

On April 13, 1972 I mailed what belongings I could, left some, and put the rest on my bicycle and pedaled the some seventy miles to the border. After crossing I stopped to clean my bike and the border patrol drove up and questioned me in regards my draft status (I lied about this as I wanted to pedal to Rockford). Five minutes later they returned to where I still was cleaning, asked me if I knew what they came back for and I said, "I guess so". I then pedaled north a little ways to Pembina, North Dakota's courthouse with them following, from there I went to the Pembina County Jail in Cavalier, North Dakota for the night (god-awful cowboy songs groaning on the radio). The next day bail was set before the U.S. Magistrate in Grand Forks, North Dakota for $2,000.00 and later I, with my bike in the trunk ("A first" says the U.S. Marshall), traveled on to Fargo's jail staying until April 18th when my mother came and posted 10% of the bond.

From May to September I worked for a wire mill as a quality control inspector 60 hours a week. In September I got shaky, left $1,000.00 at home and snuck off nervous as hell and went up to Canada for two weeks. I came back feeling like the prodigal. Now I had given myself twice a different choice and still returned and was calmer in realizing I would go through whatever would withal. Let the earth shake, my feet are planted. They wouldn't re-hire me at my old job, so I lied on an application about being arrested and got a job as a setup operator at a cardboard box factory from October to December when I quit before they fired me on hearing I was convicted. On December 5, 1972 I pleaded guilty to the charge and was placed on three years probation, two years of which would be alternative service, and two weeks in the Winnebago County Jail in Rockford, all effective January 8, 1973. The Selective Service System saw my stand finally when I was reclassified 4-F on December 27, 1972.

After doing the two weeks of incarceration in January 1973 I contacted my then probation officer, Matthew G. Ryan, and within a week got a job with Swedish-American Hospital in Rockford on the 11 p.m. to 7 a.m. shift as a unit clerk carrying out doctor's and nurses' orders and seeing to patients needs. I worked there until August 1973 when I moved to DeKalb to continue my education and married my girlfriend of 5 years on September 22nd. I did not do any alternative service from the end of August to December as I needed to pull up my grades to get off of academic probation. Starting in December I began volunteer work with the Ben Gordon Community Mental Health Center of DeKalb County as a Crisis Line telephone answerer for 50 hours a month while pursuing full-time studies through May 1974. Which brings me close to present, as I am now a houseparent (since May) providing live-in supervision and counseling for 20 mentally retarded adults at night and during the day (since October) working as a machine operator in a local lampshade factory (I no longer lie on applications).

Since conviction I have:
1. Become married.
2. Done 1¾ years of alternative service.
3. Completed 2 years probation without an arresting event.
4. Finished another year of college.
5. Paid off over $1,300.00 towards payment of school loans.
6. Purchased in full $1,080.00 for these metal-mouth braces.
7. Gotten my first car last August, a '66 Bug.

Forsooth my whole mixed-up draft life is coming to its nadir with or without pardon. I will be here till at least May this year and thus complete my two years of national good; the rest is coasting. What I ask is could I finish my two years in May 1975 then nixing that last 7 months or so of probation? Restore my liberties: Let me vote for McGovern again. I never have and will own firearms. I tried the hunting bit, shot a squirrel with a slingshot and never felt so ashamed, "Life is Sacred". Strangely it's the travel restrictions that irk me most. Calling up and being put on hold by the secretary, waiting five minutes to ask to go 10 miles North to Wisconsin. A gerrymandered age!

A lousy citizen as towards nationalism, a no go soldier for Bismarck, Ford, or any leader, steel for real I am the marrow of America's conscience and isn't this all rhetorical when I am the one who refused learning the martial arts of destruction?

A pardon without strings or leave me as is.

This has been mostly me/I don't envy your job.

May there always be,
ever something better
for which there was,
"Never More"

January 1975

6

"My Stuffed Zoo"

A house is kind of a box with many things in it. The house has many rooms. One room is my room and in it are all my stuffed animals. I like stuffed animals, the more the merrier. I think we like stuffed animals so much because people are animals too and they miss all their friends.

So when I sleep in my room all my animals watch over me and keep me company so I am never alone and have a good night's sleep and the bed bugs don't bite and I sleep tight and wake up fresh in the morning when all the animals whisper "Wake-up Annie!" and they keep on whispering louder and louder until my Mom or Dad hear something and come in my room to wake me up but then my stuffed animals are quiet because only I can hear them since in the world of make-believe there is nothing that imagination cannot do.

THE END

@1986

7

"Bounce Too Much In Scaryland"

There was a girl a boy a man a woman a dog a cat a bird a hamster and they all lived in one house one day in one year in one time when there were many monsters many nights many wolves and many scary things so so so scary that Annie the Panda said to Emily the Kangaroo let's hop out of this zoo.

And so they did again and again and again and again until they bounced their heads off and I bet that sure hurt a lot! Ouch!

THE END

@1986

8

"Our Vacation Coming Up"

There was a Mom a Dad and two sisters in one Jeep with one dog. They were on vacation and going to the mountains called the Great Smokies and then they marched through Georgia to the ocean where Annie and Emily played a whole bunch on the beach. Emily got sand in her eyes and Anna almost got bit in the foot by a crab but she didn't because she saw it in time and the crab missed.

The ocean they were at is called the Atlantic Ocean. They also took a car ferry to some islands. They camped out a lot which was fun but Mom wasn't too crazy about it. Anyway vacation was almost over and it was getting time to go home.

And this is the sad part about vacation when it is over and a happy one too when you are home again, because no matter where you are there is room in your heart for only one home. Home is not a house but where your heart is. Home is a place of mind.

THE END

@1986

9

Letter To Father

February 16, 1989

Dear Dad,

You are going to be 69 on March 13th of this year and I don't even know you.

You are drinking away the rest of your life.

You have redone your will giving everything to your new wife of 9 months and, in turn, wiped out your own children of 43 years.

When I grew up, you were either working or in the basement, so it seemed. I never could figure out what you were doing all that time in the basement, except for hiding out from Mom. Now I realize you also were drinking your hard booze too.

You never stood up to Mom's henpecks, unless you were drunk.

You submerged your feelings, desires and emotions in alcohol.

I don't think you understand what a negative impact you have made on your children's lives.

Like a rock in the pond, it is not just the splash, its effect keeps rippling outward.

I am trying to stop the ripple, the pattern created.

How do I tell you things without you getting enraged, guilty or hurt?

How do I know that what I say to you will even be remembered tomorrow, or just lost in your alcoholic stupor?

I grew up without you and I feel you will die without my ever having known you.

I understand that you have worked hard all your life at being the breadwinner, but once your work career was over you became even more lost.

I don't think that I hate you, but I can't say that I love you either.

I always told myself that I would never end up like you, not being aware that I was anyway, whether I drank or not.

I am pulling myself out of the endless low self-worth pit while watching you free-fall.
I cannot help you, I can only help myself.
I grieve for myself, I grieve for you, I grieve for the family.

Father, I never knew Ye ---

       Your Jimmy,

10

Up My Tree

The Family Tree Of
James Howard Buckingham

I will start with my Mother's history first, since my family ties tended to run stronger with the maternal side.

My Mother's Grandmother was a young Irish immigrant in the late 1800's. She died of consumption shortly after childbirth, giving birth to my Grandmother, Mae Ryan. There is no mention or knowledge of the husband or father. My Grandmother was raised by an Aunt. She married young and not much is known about the first husband other than he was an alcoholic. The relationship did not last long and she divorced him. Her son of that marriage was named Howard. She told people that her first husband was dead. She paid off the Catholic Church so she could marry again to Frank Sherman.

Frank Sherman too was an alcoholic. He had a brother who was both an alcoholic and a womanizer. The daughter of that brother now lives in her house that is chock full of everything and she never throws anything away. It is to a point that she has started to make aisles so that she can walk from room to room. She has her cat and the D.A.R. Her genealogical work has taken the Sherman family line back to General Sherman of the Civil War, David Sherman of the Revolutionary War and through wives back to the Kings of England, William the Conqueror and to Charlemagne, King of the Franks and Emperor of the West. She seems more preoccupied with our "glorious" past than with our 'glorious' present.

I never met my Mother's Father, he was an engineer for the Chicago and Northwestern Railroad and from what I gather he was a hard man. He drove the train, himself and others; his hard driving led to his death in his 50's of a heart attack.

Grandma Sherman would take turns with us kids and we would come to her house on occasion in the summer. This was a big treat for us. She had all these neat, old things. We would walk downtown to the Prince Castle for ice cream. We would walk to the next town to go swimming in the pool. Once we took the train and the bus to see a White Sox game at Comiskey Park in Chicago, picnic baskets in hand. From what I learned later, Grandma was always snubbed by Frank Sherman's mother as she felt that Grandma wasn't good enough for her boy. She was always trying to mediate fights between the family members. Grandma had high blood pressure. After her stroke, she was partially paralyzed and lost control of most of her speech. We took turns taking care of Grandma between our house and my Aunt Marilyn's. Grandma died in 1967 of another stroke.

Frank Sherman was uncomfortable with my Grandmother's son, Howard. Although Howard took on the name of Sherman, he was sent off to relatives to be raised. My Uncle Howard, my middle namesake, was a bootstrap man. He was an accountant at the First National Bank of Chicago, ending up eventually as a superintendent for a large, commercial construction firm. He loved to travel, smoke cigars and alas, drink. He loved life and idolized his Mother. He always was very busy, never having any time, "Gotta get back to work". He loved the water and had a cabin cruiser the "Why Not" on Lake Michigan for awhile. This was the man I looked up to. His first wife did not want children and wanted to move to California. He would not leave his Mother as he felt responsible for her, as she was a widow. The first wife moved on and they were divorced shortly thereafter. His second wife had three children from a previous marriage. Through the years Howard's drinking grew worse.

He was forcibly retired early from his career and it devastated him. Shortly thereafter his wife took his lump sum retirement and ran off with a boyfriend. She lost a lot of her weight. After the money ran out, the boyfriend left and she came back and so did her weight. Uncle Howard cried like a little boy at my Grandmother's funeral. Then he entered the last stages of alcoholism. He lost his driver's license. He wandered aimlessly on the city streets. In 1976 he died from cirrhosis of the liver. Uncle Howard who had been the rock for so many, would in the end, not care about himself.

Frank and Mae had three daughters by their marriage: Marjorie Jean (my Mother), Dorothy and Marilyn:
My Mother had polio when she was little and spent much time in the Shriner's Hospital. As a teenager she met my Father on a train going to

Nebraska, she never got off the seat so he wouldn't see that she was crippled. This was while my Father was in the Army during World War II. They corresponded through the war and were married when he was sent back stateside from his wound he received during the Battle of the Bulge. I guess it was what you call love at first sight. They actually only really saw each other for about three weeks prior to their marriage. My Mother didn't have the courage to tell my Father that she had polio. So when she met him at the train station when he came home from the war, he didn't know. She said he never once looked at her legs and when she said that she was crippled, he said so was he -- referring to his bandaged arm (the polio didn't matter).

I don't think my Mother ever got over having all that attention in the hospital; nor over the burden of being taunted through childhood simply because she couldn't walk right. Mom was outgoing, talkative and in charge. She was used to getting her way. Her heart was good and she both lived for and through her children. My Mother contracted asthma and allergies in her adult years. She always worked hard and worked a different shift from my Father until the kids were old enough to be without a sitter. Once all the children left, she had a hard time being with my Father, as the marital relationship had died a long time before. I felt that deep down my Mother was ashamed of my Father because he did not measure up to her city standards, not for who he was, but for what he was, a farm boy from Nebraska. In her mind, someone who was quiet was somebody awkward, not a possible virtue unto itself. The contrast between Mom and Dad grew sharper with the years and took its toll on both. My Mother was a planner, she was working towards retirement and didn't make it. She died in 1987 of asthma, at age 62.

Dorothy's nickname was Jim as her father wanted a boy. She had a very stormy relationship with her father. My Aunt Dorothy (we kids all called her "Doorknob") was very pretty in her younger years. When she married, she did not consummate the marriage. She remained living with her mother until her 30's. She always said she wouldn't even let the Pope sleep in her bed. She sought and received a Papal Annulment many years after her divorce. She idolized her half-brother Howard, like all her sisters did (as did I, more my role model I 'thought' than my own Father). She became an alcoholic and an overeater. After my Grandmother died, she moved away to Atlanta to start a new life. She was very religious. When her brother died she was found weeks later, her body floating in a river in Atlanta. I suspect she committed suicide in despair, yet it has remained a mystery. She never had children.

Marilyn was my Mom's friendly rival. She married a local boy and "did good". She was with him when he was stationed over in Germany and helped him through law school. He went on to the Legislature after becoming a lawyer. They had three children. They were the relatives we most interacted with. They were the one's who we had to keep up with. They had "it all". Aunt Marilyn's husband ended up having an affair with someone and divorced her to marry the someone. He later divorced the someone and married another. He is (was) an alcoholic. Some say the 'troubles' will find you, it's just a matter of time. My Mom's envy of Aunt Marilyn's lifestyle no longer applied. Aunt Marilyn subsequently re-married. They remained close right up to my Mom's death. Sisters-in-arms.

On my Father's side, my Great-Great Grandfather, Jesse, was a pioneer in Southwestern Iowa in the 1850's, there is some evidence that like my Mother's Father's family, they have been in this country since its beginning. The men were English and married Irish as a rule, just like on my Mother's side. Great-Great Grandfather had two wives and a total of 15 children. The second oldest child from the second marriage was my Great Grand-father.

Jesse Jr., my Great-Grandfather, sold off his share of the family farm (his inheritance) for land sight unseen in South Dakota after the Gold Rush in the Black Hills had opened up the area for white settlers, by military force. He lost his inheritance. His death certificate states that he died of heart failure in his 50's leaving behind his wife, Caroline, and 10 children, the oldest being my Grandfather.

My Grandfather, Jesse, left his native Iowa in his twenties to seek his fortune on the West Coast. There he married a woman in Spokane, Washington. The marriage did not last long. She was headstrong and they didn't get along. He came home one day from work to find her packing as she wanted to live with her parents. Grandpa said that no house was big enough for two families. She left anyway and they were divorced. Grandpa went back to Iowa. There he met my Grandmother, Eva Proffitt, while working at her father's apple orchard. They later moved to Nebraska to buy farmland.

Many years later it was discovered that Jesse had fathered a child (a girl) with his first wife. His first wife never told him. The only reason anybody ever knew was because the daughter came looking for the love of a Father since her Mother had none to give. The daughter was raised by her maternal Grandmother.

During the Depression Grandpa went to a banker to try and get a new loan, he was refused, and the banker foreclosed on the family farm. Grandpa recalled later that when he happened to be in the neighborhood, he would go call on and pay his respects to the banker; and piss on his grave. The English tradition of dry wit lived on in him.

My Father's family were very basic and survival oriented. There was no room or expense for trivial emotions. My Grandparents did not have indoor plumbing until late into their so-called retirement years; they simply kept moving the outhouse. Of the few times we went out to Gothenburg to visit my Grandparents in Nebraska, my Mother always felt she was enduring torture, as this was not what she was used to. My Grandmother had long, braided hair that she wore as a crown on her head. I only saw its true length when she would comb it out for bed. My Grandfather mowed lawns well into his eighties, eventually retiring around age 90. Grandpa always chewed tobacco. I always thought that he had tobacco juice instead of blood in his veins. He never complained and Jesse lived a full life of 103 years.

I always wondered about Grandpa's longevity. Was it simply genetic? His father died early, but his mother lived to 100. Was it the chew? The hard, rusty water from the hand pump out back? The smell from the nearby alfalfa mill that hung in the Nebraska air? Or was it his philosophy? "It is better to 'Laugh' than to 'Cry'. Work long and hard. The world is just as you make it".

Clay, my Father was the second youngest of three brothers and two sisters. Two children died in infancy. My Father was contracted out to another farmer at age 13, many miles away, where he worked for $30.00 a month plus room and board. He joined the Civilian Conservation Corps Forestry Reserves and then enlisted in the Army. During World War II he was a paratrooper with the 101st Airborne Division (the Screaming Eagles). He was wounded in the Battle of the Bulge by a machine gun from a German tank. Because of his wound he was sent home and he married my Mother shortly thereafter.

Dad didn't talk about the war much and we knew not to ask. Whenever one of us kids would be asked to wake up Dad we always tried to pass it off on someone else. The lucky one would have to touch him to wake him up and he would awake in a start screaming and yelling, arms flailing. I always thought that this was from the war, but I know that I do the same thing and so does a brother of mine, as well as, cries in the night. Neither of us have gone through a military war.

Dad was closest to my Aunt Caroline (the youngest). She seemed like a jewel in the boy's rough. She was always up, smiling and bouncy. Dad seemed to come alive in her presence and especially on visits to her farm. Dad once said that he would do anything for his sister Caroline. I didn't understand it then, I understand it now. Aunt Caroline had four children.

My Father is actually very sensitive yet he doesn't know how to show it. He only opens up when he is drunk. His forte is laconic wit, a way with words that could distill all the b.s. with one line. He has a flair for writing but not the schooling or opportunity for it. Dad has few hobbies or interests, he only knows work. Hates to travel or spend money. Now that he is retired, he is so lost. Has put all his energies into his new family of his second wife after his first wife died, to the detriment of his own.

My Mother and Father had six children:
John, the oldest, the smart one, the brain, the apple of Mom's eye. Took most of the heat from my Father's beatings. Had and still has a hard time showing any emotion. After graduating from college he joined the military intelligence in the Army. In Germany, he started with religious addiction. After the Army he went straight to California and joined a cult "The Walk". His marriage was arranged through them. A farm girl from Iowa. They have two children and still live in California and "The Walk". He and they have, more or less, completely ignored the family for years. My Mother always held out hope and it broke her heart. John, for his own reasons, had left his family for another.

Jerry, No. 2 Son, always compared to John. He could never measure up. He too, took a lot of the physical brunt of the beatings. He did not finish high school and joined up with the Army shortly thereafter. In Korea he met his wife and re-enlisted to stay over there longer. Jerry has spent his whole life running. He has been in the Army, Air Force and Marines. Spending a year or two in between enlistments in civilian life and then re-joining. Always unhappy wherever he was at. The grass was always greener. He and his wife were separated for awhile and divorce was to proceed. Asked God what he was to do and then went back to his wife. Jerry is very religious, like still water, tranquil on the surface and very deep. He needs someone to take care of him. Being too old for the military now, he works for the Post Office in Massachusetts and is currently transferring to Arizona; where things will be better. Jerry is actually a very caring person, a smashed flower.

Next is me, Jim. The sensitive one. The clown. The diplomat. the people-pleaser. Peck's Bad Boy. The rebel. The hard worker. Always working, always busy. Trying to work his way through college and not making it. Nobody was going to tell me what to do, not even the U.S. Government. Went to Canada to dodge the draft, came back, jumped bond, and came back. Out to show the world I can do it, I don't need anyone. Married his first intimate encounter. Loved children. Always playing with the younger kids. A friend to everyone, a friend with no one. Had kids to be one again, to fix it. To "Fix" his wife. To make everything OK. Left his wife and kids for his second intimate encounter. In the middle of crisis, indecision, divorce and depression and looking back for the first time in a new light. A successful business on the edge after many years of struggle. Jim has four children.

Mary, the oldest girl, Mom's favorite. Mary Jean and Jim, the two farm kids. Closest to me, next to Tom. A lot like her Mother. Incurred a lot of her Father's wrath because of same. Helped continuously by her Mother. She does not display outward signs of emotion well. Has a hard time having fun. Joined "The Walk" under the encouragement of brother John. Met her husband there. He is (was) an alcoholic. Mary had three children. The last child was while filing for divorce. She went back, it wasn't any better. After the divorce she went back again, it still wasn't better. Nobody could tell her what to do. Mary cannot relax. She has asthma and allergies. Cannot take time off for a vacation. Has not dated since her divorce seven years ago. She is starting to feel that her life has no meaning. Trying to put a focus on her own life, while raising three others on her own.

Jill, the youngest girl, Daddy's favorite. Married early. Always fixing up her house. Never has any money for anything else. Will not spend money on a vacation. Became involved in "The Walk" along with Mary and dropped out with Mary at the same time. There is a rivalry between the two sisters. The have, Jill, and the have-not, Mary. Tried to make her first husband something he was not. It didn't work. She got a divorce. Jill has two children with her second husband, who is (was) an alcoholic. Turns to her own family only when she has problems, otherwise her time is always spent with the in-laws. She once said in her first marriage that she felt more like she was a part of the in-law family then she was a Buckingham. Jill wants to reach out but stays inside.

Tom, the baby, the youngest. The one who got the best of everything. Jim's little buddy. Watched as sibling after sibling ran from the nest and left him alone. Saw more of the drinking and distance in the marriage of his parents. Cannot relax. Lots of mood swings. Hard to open up. More like Jim than the other boys. Moved out of the area after college to go to Alabama for a job at a newspaper. Saw his wife as a model for an ad in the paper. Met her at a party and courted her. They live in Florida and are expecting their first child. Again, spends more effort with the wife's family than his own. He is concerned about success. I fear for him the most of repeating my life.

This is my family. This is where I come from. There are patterns. The rest is up to me, to us, and to those who follow.

DISCLAIMER:
    As to the events, people and descriptions mentioned above, these are only what I either know of or have been told. In the final analysis, this is my viewpoint and not necessarily as to the whole truth of the matter, which may never be known. No aforethought of malice whatsoever is intended as to the parties. Only love is intended in trying to describe and explain my heritage. All errors remain mine.

Summer 1989
Winter 1995 Revised & Corrected, Not Updated

11

A Modest Proposal for The Faint of Heart

The advance of modern medicine is continually opening the door to new frontiers. What was unheard of or pioneering 20 years ago is now common-place. In the area of heart transplants (natural), survival rates have improved. With the decline of expectations towards the artificial heart, natural heart transplants remain the best approach to date; the one glitch remains, supply. The amount of donors falls far short of demand. In spite of widespread use of donor cards and the options of presumed consent and required request, demand still outstrips supply.

What I propose is other unexplored avenues to address this need. Since the heart is merely a circulatory organ, for which no artificial substitute has been found, one must look at the untapped pool available. Certain archaic restrictions stand in place as to the full use and benefit of medical science today. That a man in the prime of his life, at age 55, should not have a donor heart when his is failing due to lifelong habits of smoking, obesity and inactivity screams of indecency. Odds are this same man could live another five years or more before he needed another transplant. Are we not asking too much of the dead or terminally ill, that since their demise is a foregone conclusion, now it is time for them to prolong another's life? Why all this namby-pamby about the respect for the dead or their survivors? Do the departed need a warm heart for those cold winter nights? Will they suffer loss in future relationships or miss not having something to gladden? Let us take off the gloves of civility. We are not talking about religion, we are talking about science, by God!

Then I say, let us move forward in the name of science without people standing and obstructing the path. What areas have not been explored? Many, many. It is only the limit of our resourcefulness as to how far we need to go to correct the problem. I can begin with prisons. Surely a

prisoner on death row would consider an alternative to festering in his/
her cell. How about five years of freedom before you get fried, hung,
gassed or injected? Why waste a resource? Incentive is a powerful thing.
Immediate organ procurement could follow euthanasia and still leave the
shell. Most would maintain that a death row prisoner is but a shell anyway.
Don't we do the same for dogs who are in pain and misery? Didn't
the Aztecs have something similar in how well they treated their human
sacrifices up to their appointed time? A reduction in prison costs would
be a desired side effect.

What about those consent forms? Does the feelings or belief of a dead
individual outweigh the overall good of society? We are talking about the
pieces of a whole, the sum is greater than the parts. When you take away
a part or parts of a dead sum, what you still have is a dead sum, more
or less. Isn't it time we started to look at life more analytically and get a
better view of things? Mandatory organ procurement can be controlled
by the government. The sales alone could wipe out the budget deficit and
make us a trader surplus nation and elevate us back to our former glory.

There are many other creative ideas to consider. Why abort fetuses?
Give the mother a generous subsidy, birth it and do the procurements.
Other alternatives are wrong sex, preemies or birth defects, etc. and even
if the brain is damaged, is not the heart or other parts still good? Why
should we limit ourselves to any less of a potential then extending human
life wherever possible? If we can expand the range of human life to 100
or 110, then let's do it, the cost is irrelevant. I could go on, but time
dictates I slow down my digression -- as long as -- you get the point.

Remember what legally decides human life is whether your brain is
working or not. If your brain doesn't work, you have no life. And without
life, you cannot feel or see things as they are. The greatest scientific minds
of our time were not hindered by emotion. Would we have the atom bomb
today if Dr. Oppenheimer had thought of anything except his field of
science? Throw away your selfish concerns and sign away your heart, for
the heart you save will not be your own.

February 22, 1990

12

Retreat

QUESTIONS:

1. Why am I here? What are my feelings right now about being here?

2. What are my feelings about this weekend? What are my hopes about this weekend?

3. What am I willing to do to make this weekend serve me?

1. Why am I here? Because I feel I still have leftovers in my fridge. That despite all that has gone before, part of me still feels missing. The separation with my children, the old dreams that died hard, the resistance to God's hand.

My feelings about being here are ok Even though I have 10 tons of things to do. The time I need is right here and now. I first must be for myself, this is the hardest for me, let me worry about others; but not about me.

2. My fear for this weekend is opening up the grave once more. How many times must I still cry? Does it end with passing or simply grow fainter? Can I put the past in its place? Do I still drift towards being stuck in the past, worrying about the future and pissing on today?

My hope is to open up more and more. Let God in. Let love in. There is pain, there is hurt. Life is not without these. But to also look at the good. To not only say, but to feel, my glass is half full not half empty. I am on my way. I do not know where. That is God's job, not mine. If I can quit playing God then maybe God would say, "OK, Jim now it's your turn to be who you are. Not somebody's something. Just you. Have faith. Just be and I will be with you."

3. Be open. To share. No judgments, no all knowing sage advice. That my experience might help someone or that their's should help me.

Time to reflect. Look back, look forward, live and let live. Easier said than done. But essential. Like forgiving.

To forgive someone, I must first forgive myself. To work on forgiveness, to clean my heart out so my soul is lighter from the dust of guilt, anxiety and sadness.

QUESTIONS:

1. What masks do I wear? How do I feel when I wear these masks?

2. What are my good qualities? How do I feel about these good qualities?

3. What pretenses do I bring into my relationships with my fellow workers, children, friends, etc.?

4. What personal strengths do I bring into my relationships with my fellow workers, children, friends, etc.?

1. I wear the mask of confidence when I don't feel confident. I wear the mask of affability when I don't want to please that person. I wear the mask of silence when I need to talk out. I wear the mask of calm when I am mad. I wear the mask of guilt when I need to be there for myself. I wear the mask of quiet suffering and martyrdom when I have been betrayed, let down, lied to, disregarded and ignored.

All these masks keep me from being me and after wearing them so long from childhood on, I have to keep peeling them away, opening one box after another, only to find still another box inside.

I have my baby picture (3-4 months old) hanging in my bedroom and I look at that rolly-polly little boy with such a great head of hair and a great big, natural smile and I say, "God, that's me!" What happened? Though life isn't just a nursery rhyme, I continue searching for that same child inside me. The perfect oneness with myself. Free expression. No apprehension. No guilt. No pain. There is today. Contentment in one's own self.

2. I am a very thoughtful person and perceptive about a lot of things, unless I am personally involved. I am smart and a good friend and lover. I enjoy the quiet things of life and nature's beauty as wrought by God. I look for the simpler essence if my penchant for complication doesn't start interfering. I love my children almost more than I love myself and I hope to be a better person, father and husband in my next chapter in life.

I am day by day feeling better about myself rather than putting myself down or replaying old, negative tapes. The one drawback of my good qualities is to do to excess. To think of others needs first rather than my own at times and conversely to just think of myself when I should be including others; a delicate balance that I need to work on.

3. That everything is fine because I have not raised any immediate objection. For too long I have sat upon the quiet rock. Instead of voicing my opinion, I withhold. Then I think about it more and more and I get mad and/or resentful or simply brush it aside saying, "it's no big deal", when in actuality it shouldn't be tolerated. Taking too long to act and worrying about how others will feel and not about my own feelings. I need

to stand up more for myself, to be at least one-half the protector of my needs and desires as much as I am for others.

4. To get the job done. To take charge. To orchestrate. To make plans. To get together. To make it happen. To bring harmony and a sense of belonging. To pitch in and roll up my sleeves; don't talk about it, *just do it.*

QUESTIONS:

1. Describe the stages where I have been and am in my life, in the stages of grief:
DENIAL:
RESENTMENT:
BARGAINING:
RESIGNATION:
ACCEPTANCE:

DENIAL: That despite whatever transpired, happened or amount of time passing, or even a divorce, that eventually it would all work out again and the "original" family would be whole once more. That I would be with my kids everyday, no more back and forth, that I could tuck my kids in at night and read them a story and do things and plan things and keep everyone happy.

Now I am divorced and though you hear it, and it happens, it is few and far between that people remarry each other after they divorce. And if they do, was it really for the right reason, or simply fear of starting anew? Hanging on for what?

I am divorced and though I am not proud of it, I am proud of myself. I finally did not give in or give up, I gave in to God's will, not my own, for even at the bitter end I had not the heart to finish it; and she mocked me in disdain. I held God's hand and humbly walked with Him. There is no denying a marriage of 15 years is done and putting the lid on its coffin, lest the worms come crawling out.

RESENTMENT: Where do I begin? That she never wanted our beautiful babies. That three of those babies never breathed life but were sucked to death and snatched from her wicked womb. That I did not stand up earlier or stand for my convictions. That she got fatter and fatter as a means to keep a sexual distance and since that didn't work, she just ate more. The constant nagging, that I never did anything to help her around the house or with the little kids, since she had to work (2-3 days a week), compared to my 50-60 hours a week to make more money, because there never was enough. Never enough food to cram down her throat. Never enough distance to keep me away. Never enough times that I was not repulsed from her anger at again being inconvenienced in the marital bed. She was not "My sleeping pill!"

Her coldness. Her lack of enthusiasm. And then once I was gone, she was the poor, suffering madonna, the pregnant woman left in the lurch by the gallivanting heel off with another woman. Left destitute by the husband who paid all the bills while he slept on the office floor, who did not pay his own bills on time so that the marital bills would get paid.

So she went on a drastic diet on my insurance to lose weight and she got her tubes tied for no more babies; now I couldn't get her pregnant. It was no longer my responsibility. Now she wanted her Friday nights free to socialize when she always worked Fridays so I could stay home with the kids. Now she didn't care about the house, when that is what all that seemed to matter. Now she liked camping and bicycling and everything else she grudgingly came along on in the family outings and even before we had kids as a reluctant, bitchy grumbler. You want resentments, I had 'em!

And now, well I finally either saw the light and have left behind one hell of a sick woman or maybe it's as simple as this: she likes it better alone or she likes it better without me. Nobody to answer to. Nobody to confront. No pressure for sharing, touching or kissing. Do as you please and still get $250.00 a week child support in the same house, same furniture and same dog, and when the kids are gone with Dad, free time and free baby-sitting. She now works full-time (I put her through nursing school) but hey, what price freedom? The price was our marriage. That for many a reason, we were never really there on both parts. Two people hanging on to a mismatch, denying different emotional levels and masking it all with high intelligence as they both went crazier and crazier in their own separate lives.

BARGAINING: God take away the pain, help me make a decision, should I get divorced or not? Sue or Lou? Lou or Sue? Lou or nobody? Sue or nobody? Nobody or nobody? Anybody or nobody? Help me, help me, help me!

What about the kids, how are they doing? Are they okay? Who is watching them? What are they thinking? How can I make it right? What is happening? I can't take much more of this, I am obsessing.

Maybe if I go on a trip with Sue I'll feel better. I'll buy more things for Lou. I'll just keep putting everybody off: Sue, Lou and the lawyers. I gotta' hang on a little longer. Maybe Jesus will come to me and tell me what to do. I need more time. I need to make more money. I need to buy time. Everything is building up. What seemed easy is now very, very hard.

My bargain was money. I gave Mary Lou the last of her free maintenance in July. I paid for Lou's airfare to Montana for a rugged camping trip in August and left her a $100.00 bill for spending money. I blew apart my own vacation with Sue and the kids to race back to her, to wait for her.

RESIGNATION: And now the party was over. The money tree was dry. There was no more. And the madonna was strong and cold as ice, I should quit bothering her. She had her taste and she liked it. If I couldn't finish what I had started, she would she said, as she looked at me with a smirk of disgust on her face at having to dispense with such a weak man who she had no respect for.

So in the final hour I let go. I admitted defeat and died and my world of illusion fell apart. I was the actor and the play was ending. I had to do it all, alone. The courtroom was empty, the words final and hollow, it was over and clinically dead. I went back to my little apartment and cried for three hours straight. Straight from the gut of my soul. I left October 21, 1988 and now was divorced on September 19, 1989 just 3 days short of a 16th anniversary. And God held me tight, for irregardless of a new relationship, I felt alone in my grief.

So I'm divorced! I'm panicking! I can still fix it! I send her 15 red roses on the 16th anniversary. We go for a bike ride. Maybe we can get back together. But everytime I see some of the ugliness I had swept under the rug. She is interested in others too and it is easier for her to try someone else than deal with us, me or her, our problems that are now so evident.

ACCEPTANCE: And with time, even without my always being aware, I let go and let go. I leave her alone, so I can go on as well.

QUESTIONS:

1. What trust means to me is ...... In light of this definition, how do I trust myself? How do I trust others?

2. To whom do I go to share my deepest feelings? What feelings do I find easy to share with others? What feelings do I find most difficult to share?

3. What are my feelings about involving myself physically and intimately in sexual relationships? How do these feelings relate to my personal values?

1. What trust means to me is placing my best interests in somebody else's care that would not be violated; I would be treated by them as they in turn would like to be treated, a sort of do unto others.

I do not trust myself enough because self-doubts and misgivings keep getting in the way. I do not always think highly of myself enough to watch out for my own best interest. Instead, I look out for the other guy and worry about them when that may or may not be in my interest also. I am working on it and I have a long way to go.

I have problems trusting others. Because of past experience in betrayal as a child from my parents and with all my brothers and sisters being busy looking out and scrambling for themselves, I grew up with guarded trust.

Even in my relationship with Mary Lou the pattern was repeated and intensified.

Betrayal, lies and withdrawal. Never knowing where I am at and how I stand. Now with Sue I am tested to my own definition, can I break or repeat my patterns? Am I so concerned about my own and others lack of success that I fear failure more than anything? I have learned and am still learning to trust in God and His Will be done, for surely my willfulness made my life amok. I have to balance between blind, unfounded trust and invested trust. That which has earned and is safe. That to live a life, I must start trusting and risk by sharing a trust to start anew.

2. First with God, for He already knows, and gradually with Sue, my confidante. Easy feelings to share are the light ones: happy, grumpy, the one's on the outer surface. The more difficult things to share are my innermost thoughts, fears, anxiety, pain, trauma and shame.

3. Good, now I am born anew and this shame in my past is now gone. I can hug and be hugged, kiss and be kissed, touch and be touched, snuggle and be snuggled and after twenty years of trying to make love to a woman I can have an orgasm that I didn't get by myself alone.

The new intimacy is relaxed, easygoing, fun, joyful and playful. There is no fear of rejection or thoughts of maybe this week, or what about tonight, or will she be in the mood? Or maybe if she was happier she could enjoy it too?

My personal values affirm my late blooming sexuality. It is natural and right. Sometimes it scares me even to think how sexual I am. I am "not" a sex maniac or sexually addicted. This is just me and it is right and good. God doesn't make crap. Mary Lou is and was Mary Lou. Sue is and was Sue. Sexual mismatch and leave it be. Probably sounds too simple, but true.

I need to be me, trite and true. For falsehood became myself suppressed in a continually, debasing shame to enable my survival in an unhealthy relationship for me. That I must not forget and that I do not miss. And for this, if nothing else, I thank the Lord, my God, for my deliverance.

P.S. And I pray for my children, for their "mental", sexual and physical health and that they might be spared some of the HELL I have gone through, and even more so for their children.   Amen

QUESTIONS:

1. Looking back over my life, what are some personal experiences that convince me of God's presence and care for me?

2. How has my relationship with God modified or evolved since I have been alone?

3. Have I experienced the unconditional love of God in my life? If so, in what ways?

1. Not being run over by a snowplow when it started to back up, both when I was a child and as an adult. Not being killed in my motorcycle accident. Staying away from suicide in my despair. Watching over me while I was in Canada and in jail. The gift of my lovely children. The signals to me from my Mother's death. The stop to my self-destruction in my first marriage. How my divorce got me back to God and away from playing God. How my sickness has awakened me to my asthma. How tragedy can turn into a reward. For the baptism of my four children on Easter Sunday 1990.

2. Yes, it has been reborn anew, one step beyond the rote, blind faith as a child to a new adult blind faith and love of His wisdom. That every time has a meaning and neither to second guess or presume that I can always make things right, nor make things turn out my way. One day at a time. One step at a time. To stand up for what I believe.

3. Yes, on coming back to the church in the depths of my crisis (divorce) I was lower than low and subject to rejection or judgment from the church. It was not there. In the confessional it was an affirming and a welcome back home; and that has opened many doors that I may have otherwise gone blindly by, never knowing in my haste and madness, and for this I am grateful to God. Although I cannot make the world right, "I can stop the pain and hurt", first with me and then hopefully with others in time.

QUESTIONS:
1. What are the things which make me feel the most guilty?
2. Which are unrealistic guilts? Which are realistic guilts?
3. How do I feel about these guilts?
4. How can I forgive myself of these guilts, and then be free? How do I feel about forgiving myself?

1. Survivor's Guilt. That I am out of the former family situation and do not have my children with me. To care for, protect and daily nurture my children.

2. Realistic: To not keep putting things off. To have more honest, direct and open confrontations in a beneficial conflict sense, rather than a one-upmanship, who wins/who loses; controlling and push and pull behavior, taking for granted. How it happened and the timing.

Unrealistic: Was it avoidable? Could reconciliation have worked? Someone would change. It was all my fault. If only. If only.

3. Working on 'em. I am not a savior. I am not a saint. I am tired of going over the same dead-ends, my eyes are bloodshot from looking at my life under a microscope. Such scrutiny is neither plausible nor sustainable.

4. Letting go. Being honest. Forgiving Lou. To forgive myself.

QUESTIONS:

1. Write a closure letter to your former spouse. Or, what are my feelings about "Closing the door gently" on the marriage?

2. How do I want to go on living?

3. How can I begin to see and accept myself...as I really am today?

1.   July 1, 1990

Dear Mary Lou,

I wish I had brought the poem with me that I had written to you last January. The words said back then still hold true. My favorite line was towards the end about the children, "being the best of both could be".

So much has come and gone since I didn't come home that October night. For eleven years you anticipated that one day, how I would not return. And in that time you forgot about us (as I also), and we didn't come first. And so your fears came true by perpetuating the dread. How much of a part do we play through our own acts?

Yet the river of life moves on. Lest we all get stuck in some backwater and stagnate. Both of us, each in their own ways, have been going on and making changes. I know there have been times (and I'm sure there will be more to come) when our anger boils to the surface. Like the time in Yellowstone by the geysers, the gas bubbled to the surface with the smell of sulfur in the air, the stinkpots.

As in all memories, one can pick out what one will. Good, bad or indifferent they remain that, memories. Living in today for tomorrow is not possible for the past. We still have many years of co-parenting together. I know my struggle is in not having the children and your's is in having them. I hope to keep that conflict in control, and to be understanding enough of you if you should finally decide to let them go; and to accept my role peacefully if that never comes to pass.

That line of my poem now applies equally to us, "being the best each could be".

> Good Luck,
> Jim

2. My Goals for Living:

1. To keep in touch with God.
2. To love myself.

3. To love my new spouse Sue as myself, not more, not less.

4. To keep my love alive with my children without smothering them, and to be understanding, short of acting on guilt.

5. To foster love in all I meet.

6. To work on friendships, their strength is an armada.

7. To be a helpful and not an enabling hand to friends and relatives in their proper place, and this even would include Mary Lou.

8. To look back proudly on my life's accomplishments, not in material or money, but through the heart and mind, as I have touched people on my way.

3. I am a sensitive person, rather oversensitive. Recently I learned I have asthma, so I am being desensitized by allergy shots. I need to deprogram my antennae which are always sticking way up high, looking and checking for any signals.

That I am a hell of a guy and it is ok to think that way, short of being pompous. That I don't have the slightest idea or inkling of what might happen to me tomorrow or ten or twenty years from now and that's fine too.

One has to work with what you've got. We are all Popeye's. "I am what I am." As long as that am is really you. Not your parents, guardians, relatives, spouse or kids, but YOU. That is hard, this is a life goal.

That I am a Buckingham, I am God's child, I am proud. It is time to lay down the gavel, no longer to hit myself over the head with, no longer to spew dissension, let God judge alone. My role is to be, not preside. Life can be easier, if only we let it happen that way.

Notes from the Beginning Experience Retreat on June 29 - July 1, 1990

13

Caroling for Christine

I walked with my daughter, Emily Christine, across the way to go to CCD. The bells in the carillon were ringing as we went by Saints Peter and Paul and I immediately thought of the Angelus for Vespers. As I walked back the bells played on. And for the moment I reached back to the ancestry of a connected age where all order was preordained and the sacredness of life embosomed your soul.

But now we are smarter and we are know better. And we have lost the God in ourselves and our world around. The only mystery remaining is what science has yet to discover to add to our faith in man alone. Still the disillusion and despair of the modern age will go on until we awake from our amnesia with the past. A past that remains everywhere if we can just see, if we can just hear, if we can just touch and allow the feeling.

The key to complexity is simple, the answer for strife is ease. God did not intention us to race to our death, to hurry our passing and not look around. What do you have that you do not need? What do you want that you think you must have? Does all of your work satisfy your longings? And for how long? The desire of the spirit is unquenchable in meeting with the God in everyone and everything. We could be the Dracula of the Ages and never cease our nightly prowls to drink of the knowledge of all. With the fruit of desire came the need to know and a certain emptiness of never finishing the task.

So who is the wiser? The common man or the learned one? For all learning is not knowledge when it comes to faith. Faith is exercised every day in your own being. So take, grab and hold that faith of children that holds without question. Listen to the bells as they play their music, as you hold your daughter's warm hand; to take her to a teaching of a tradition to pass through her as it was through you. As your parents' blood coursed through you, so now does your's pulse through your child. That as in long ago, but not so long that it cannot still be felt today, though a continent and centuries away. Hold your head in reverence to your field in life, all life, and to those around you and give thanks and praise that we may share with one another and be a part of this life that goes on; which is our hertitage and the heritage of us that we pass along.

How many have you touched in how many ways? What is your legacy? Your legacy is you and no other. What have you given up personally? How many people share in the ownership of yourself? How many things own you and have become your God to which you give daily homage? What course have you set for the stewardship over your body, your family, your fellow man and that of the earth that you temporarily have dominion? What will remain from the wake you leave behind?

Sing out for yourself, your loved ones, an understanding love for your enemy, a compassionate love for those in need, a jealous love for your home of Earth, and a sacred love for all life and from Whom all things owe. Be at one with yourself, stop and say your prayer to God and be part of the reverence in life. Touch again, be alive, as I hold my daughter's hand and love her so and that for all our troubles in the moments of our lives, I sing the praise of my daughter through myself and from my God. That life is an endless miracle.

September 5, 1991 A.D.

14

The Wedding Vase

I heard a story in my father's house of a young couple who passed by St. Francis Cathedral on their way to the Indian market on the plaza. As the bells chimed, calling the faithful, they perused the wares hawked by the impassive sellers. Arm in arm they walked uncaring and unknowing of their life ahead of them and the future they created with each day.

The young man spotted a display that beckoned his eye and asked, "What are these?"
"Wedding Vases." replied the Indian.
"What are they for?"
"They are for Life and Marriage."
"Great, we're on our honeymoon. It'll make a neat souvenir!"
"Take care not to break the two handles."
"OK. Wrap it up good will ya, we've got a long way to go home."
"The vase is fragile, hold it carefully - lest you destroy it, for there is much power between two people."

The young woman thought how quaint! Here was this wrinkly wizen of an Indian dispensing wisdom like candy out of a Pez dispenser. More likely, a way of throwing people off guard so they won't haggle for a better price. The vase was wrapped up carefully in newspaper and wrapped again for shipping. The Indian said he would take care of everything and not to worry until they got home and put the vase on the shelf and then time would be talking.

All things considered, the rest of the trip went fairly well. Only a few fights, nothing that couldn't be overlooked, patched up later, smoothed over for now or best forgotten in the deep, dank trunk of musty memories mired with silent unhappiness.

And another life began. A married couple. Each starting with different agendas, backgrounds and hopes and dreams to settle upon a different way. The vase stood on a shelf made with bricks and boards, an artsy-fartsy config for sure, but cheap, homemade and sensible. And the accumulations of impediments knocked on their door. They opened the door together, smiled and welcomed the parade right in. The march began slowly for money was short, but hopes were high for more and better. Or which was it, better or more? A sofa, a chair, a bike, a canoe, a car, another vacation, more clothes, a baby, dishes, a table, a rocker. Did I say baby?

What was so easy became difficult now that the couple was gone. Family came first. The baby needed many, many things. A walker, a stroller, a carriage, a playpen, a car seat, a bike seat, a crib, a changing table. Mind you the baby never actually asked for these things, but you could tell. Mostly the baby needed to be held. To be loved. The baby swing cut down on the holding part a lot. And the pacifier, they called it a blooper, cut down on the crying and the talking. Solo babies are rarely balanced in arms, so along came more.

The vase went from bricks and boards to a fireplace shelf, a china cabinet, a corner cupboard, to the back room den, and finally ended up in a forgotten box in the attic. The ceramic had many cracks with age and a few chips from misuse and now was packed in the very paper it originally came in. The couple had gone from hand-to-hand to a steely distance. They were surrounded by many things in their home and they truly had nothing.

Then one day a great wind came in and blew into their lives and tore open the facade they made and kept, exposing the rotten framing behind. You see there was a small hole in the roof of their understanding. At first they didn't even know what was there. But after awhile they could no longer ignore it. A stain was starting to show. The remedy was a bucket that was emptied in secret on occasion. This was better than fixing the problem, for neither could they find the trouble nor agree as to how the trouble started. The problem had grown so large that repair seemed no longer the word. There was more work in emptying the bucket than letting go. After a long time someone forgot about the bucket.

After the wind had blown away, the waters washed over the ruins. What was left was the former couple, their children, and many, many possessions that now no longer seemed to be of matter. In a pique of anger the woman ran to the box containing the wedding vase and hurled it at the man. The final impact sundered the vase into a thousand pieces. And the man left with a stolen fragment of the broken vase.

More seasons had come and gone and now the same man strolled from St. Francis Cathedral after Mass, and arm in arm with his new love, came upon the plaza. The sun hung high and hot and the roof of the earth was blue with a dab or two of white puffs here and there. Today was a day of senses and justification for being.

They walked on past the Indians in a row with their crafts in front of them arrayed on the blankets on the sidewalk. As they passed the wedding vases the middle-aged man stopped and turned toward the seller. There sat the same old man, he was sure! Memory be fooled, if time didn't seem the same. Was his journey a circle? As he started to talk, the Indian said,
"I'm sorry, these are not for sale."
"Why not?" the man asked somewhat indignant, ready for anger to bubble.
"Only one to a customer."
"I don't have one!"
"Yes you do. Take it out of your jacket."
"But," the man started to protest, yet sheepishly pulled out of his inside breast pocket the one shard he still had from the wedding vase he had lost so long ago.

The Indian took the piece, spat on it, and hit the clay with a hammer making a small cloud of smoke. He then took the powder and breathed on it and brushing the man's jacket to the side, reached into the man's heart and pulled out the same, perfect wedding vase from years past. He held up the vase to the Sun in front of the man's eyes and proceeded to put the vase back into the man's heart.

He then spoke,
"I gave you this long before and told you to be careful. I give you your vessel back again and show you that you always have this in you. The true care and container of love is yourself and no other."

The man shook himself as from a deep trance, where one is when you are far away and not here and now. He smiled, shook his head and said,
"You're right. I have one already. Thank You."
He walked on by. And the Indian said in calling,
"My peace be with you brother."

And that is how my Father told me the story of HIS Sante Fe heart.

May 30, 1993

15

Walk with the Woollies

As the father and mother curled back to their charges, they chimed in unison: "Remember children, stick together."

Just then the loud roar from the sky arose and breezed by ever so quickly.
After the noise was gone, one child said:
"What was that?"
"That was the great black squisher" said the father.
"Many has been the woolly who never made it across."
"Why, why?" all the children wanted to know.
The mother then took her turn,
"Some felt they didn't need any help.
Some lost their way, their courage.
They forgot what it was all about."

"Is it who can get there first?"
"Who has the finest fur?"
"How much you can bring with you?"
"They didn't concentrate enough on the other side?"
"Enough, enough" the mother chuckled, "Let your father finish the story."

"As your mother said, this is not just a walk to the other side.
It is your fine walk in the sun.
Keep your hearts set for the other side.
Yet there is much more and a lot less.
Stay true to your self and each other.
How you walk will be remembered for all time.
What you do on the way will affect others.
Remember the journey's the thing."

Puzzlement was written all over the kid's hairs and a sense of worry now took hold. All the legs front to rear collided after hearing their parents words. None wished to go forward anymore. The ambitious child started out tentatively and curling back waved the others forward with his antennae.

"Well mom? Well dad? Aren't you coming?"

"No dear, our time is done. You go ahead."

"But we can't leave you both, we need you!"

"You'll be just fine, go on now."

"Will we see you again?"

"Of course you will, we will see you on the other side."

"Good Luck, God Speed, We Love You All!"

"We Love You Too Mom and Dad!"

With that the children were on their way.
A short time later they heard a roar behind them, where their parents were.
A few of the kids paths intersected with each other now and then.
Some journeyed together for awhile.
Others went alone.
As they each went they met others on the way.
And they had a lifetime on that day.

In the end was the other side.
And their parents were there just like they said.
So too were many others, friends and relatives,
Some from long ago, others met just in passing.
Everyone talked and laughed and sang.
Not all made it.
The reason wasn't the black squisher.
Everyone met the black squisher.
There was no way around it.
Some barely put ten feet on the road and along came the roar.
Others went back and forth for many times until the end.
The squish came when the squish came,
To worry about it was silly.

What kept quite a few from getting to the other side,
was that when the squish came upon them,
the black was inside them.
That black was because there was no light inside them.
And when their walk was done it was too late.
They all seemed so surprised when the roar was for them.

To this day the talk among the woollies is this:
"If your walk is not a good one,
You will have to keep doing it again and again.
Some poor souls have been walking over and over for a long, long time.
Some have been taken away from the walk period,
Never having learnt a thing,
Now they look only at misery and regret."

Remember the walk is your walk and what you do with it is your decision.
As woollies come and go with each season,
As the robins come in the spring,
As colors turn beautiful green and flaming red,
As the geese and the cranes fly north and south each year,
With each rise and fall,
Celebrate Life,
Celebrate Death,
You need both to get to the other side.

P.S. If on a sunny day in the fall you see somebody weaving down a
warm, country blacktop in the heartland don't assume that the person driving has had too much to drink, is in convulsions, or having
a problem.

Perhaps it is simply because the driver is weaving in and out of the
woolly caterpillars on the road, so that they may not meet their black
squisher that day.

February 20, 1994

Mother and Father Wedding Day April 21, 1945

Jerry, Jim, Mary, Mom, Jill and John Easter Sunday 1959

Dad, John, Mom, Tom, Jim, Jill, Jerry and Mary
1966

John, Mary, Jim, Jill and Jerry Christmas 1955

John's Seventh Birthday at Grandma Sherman's 1953
Aunt Marilyn, Mom, Dad, Mary, Aunt Dorothy, Jim, Jerry, John
and Grandma

Grandpa and Grandma Buckingham on a visit East

Emily, Anna, Dad and Will Easter Sunday 1988

Storyteller to his children

Jim and Sue Wedding Day August 11, 1990

~ Part II ~

Songs To Sing

Seasonal People

It is very cold.
With the damp pushing down
the shivers on the back of you.
And you close in to gather your troops,
to mount your sword,
to fend for yourself;
bound the puddles and manoeuvre
the corpus to avoid wetness to the parts.

Water shows more,
points out the dirt,
laughs at the scrub brush.

"We all fear."

Tighten up, clamp more gates.
More for 1, less for 2.
Really,
        we are very cold people,
only warm when,
waiting for the nother, next, rain.

1969

born to be ground

squeamy squirmy wormy
wriggling all about
waiting to be stepped on
it waits without a doubt

squeamy, squirmy, and wormy
wriggling all about
"poor little man" reflects on
his hated turnabout

1969

What Happens?

What is it like on the night
of no moon
with no stars seen because of
clouds on the top,
and no lights are near?
What is like when the electricity
fails on a cold day
and we are snowed in
when the oil is gone,
the coal no more,
the water too brackish
and the air too thick
with poison too high?
Absurdity.

1969

A Lingering Day

I lie in bed
and feel sunken in,
the pillow, mattress and covers
envelop me,
I don't want to rise.
I only wish to keep
my existence like this:
a soothing drowsy semisleep
with no worry, no pain,
and no meaningful thoughts.

To get up
to stay,
to live
to die -----
all the same -- no difference.

1969

Attending to the burial of the philosophical deities of man, and man

"O sophisticate gods of the unexplainable!
You are my explanation.
My vision in the crystal ball
that I wanted to see."

Sum, Cogito, Sapiens.
I am, I think, wise ---

And the words are my biased own
that I made up to suit a purpose,
like you,
so I can think myself splendid
in the limited physics
of light's speed
and the universe.

And a round coffin
is crawling with crabby cockroaches
and their own crumbling colossus to themselves.

Being laid down
and dressed up
is but a comfort
to the dead of Mind.

1969

"Artson Son of Art"

Of a great man and a small land we speak
near the glacial lake of Michigan,
neath the concrete structures and breweries
amidst the blue brows of sweat and ignorance,
Artson Son of Art carved of the city
a stone face with Zoroaster eyes.
Artson Son of Art was not to be
a greater fate was in store for he.

Born of mediocrity and standard balls
on a quiet street under anormal sky
poor Artie said "Why?"
The kings of the land were not for he
one of the kings he's gonna pee.

The churn of education promised him solace
and he became a janitor/waiter of prowess,
wasting away the hours
for a girl who might iron his collars;
not a kiss, not a goose
what's the sense of this moose?
He shaved his head, combed his ass
she still wouldn't celebrate the conjugal mass
but farted.

Artson sought a way out of this time:
to destroy and create with one ejaculative stroke
the "meaning" of life, what a joke!
So he went to the shop and bought a new cock
and lined it with six new bitters.

Summer 1972 in collaboration with Craig Campbell
(One of the Soup Brothers)

Mom's Eulogy

Dear Mom,
Mom, you are the happy wanderer.
From the wilds of Canada
to the Rocky Mountains
to the Emerald Isle
and to points far and near.
You sought delight
in God's natural wonders,
you sought life.

You have gone on
to other trips
where we have yet to follow.
We all hope to find
your blazes of generosity,
concern and well-meaning
on the trail.
You have left us sadder
for now
our sadness will change
to fond remembrances.

A free spirit
and a can do person.

You breathe freely now.
We love you.

-- Go with God --

August 1987

For every time there is a Season

That a crop should not renew
continually in the field
does not bespeak ill
of the planter or the seed's yield

Rather, remember every time
the harsh winters, the long summers
and the rising and falls
in between and asunder

Sometimes the soil and crop do well
and then gradually, one does not know when
the yield and the plenty subsides
and the farmer moves on, to toil again

Although the land does heal
and the farmer fondly remembers
he knows to go back is false
when the labor of love has died in the embers

Still the land produced fruit
which were bountiful and good
and the fruit continues on
as the best of both ever could

For every time there is a Season.

January 1989

"Stolen Moments"
A Sunday at Starved Rock

Cruisin' in from Chicago
we got in about two a.m.,
another harried weekend
but that's
how it's always been.
Quick, unload and check-in
get settled and undressed.
And the maiden rides her pony
and the minstrel plows his field
the Earth loves the Sun
the Sun loves the Earth
Apollo and Diana
together at last.
And now some rest.

Drawing back the curtains
of what was pictured as dark
is now a bright day.
Get dressed and load up
time to check out.
And after brunch,
hiking sticks in hand,
we do our walkabout.

We come upon a man
and his wife
their children and dog
and a ferret
named Rat
who are sledding down the slope
of a Rock that echoes
the sound of a dying tribe.
And upon that Rock
on this beautiful day
it is hard to say
what tribute one can offer
to those people that died here
and forever
marked this spot.

Continuing on
we absorb the energy
of old Mr. Sol
like bouncy, little children
on a playground lot.
The snow was all coated
with a skin of icing
that crunched underfoot
as we made
our slippery way.
And had some fun,
sliding down knolls
on a sled called
the Butt.

Up at Eagle Cliff Overlook
was a couple from Aurora
taking a domestic break
from painting and chores
renewing their own
energy stores.
The water of the Illinois
spilling over the dam
what a sight to see.
Makes me wanna' pee!

The boys from Sandwich
were all hollerin'
down below
venting their steam
in Wildcat Canyon
amongst the ice
and the snow.
And we wrastled
and rolled around
crumbling cookies
in our backpacks
on the ground.

It was time for dinner
and the hostess said, "Hi.
Are you from Caterpillar?"
To which I replied,
"No, but I can crawl
if you want me to."
Now we were coming
to the end of our day
saying good-bye to
the Indians
the Fleur de Lis
the Union Jack
the Stars and Stripes
and the Illinoisy.

Time to go back
to work, bills and taxes
and the everyday
of the responsible masses.
And to keep the love
with my children,
my issue.

So we squeezed it in,
the precious time,
Like raindew drops
on a spider's web
early in the morn'
Double rainbows in the sky
Shared laughter
A baby's smile
All these times
make a pot of gold possible
at the end of your rainbow.

For time does not steal
it is, was and will.
Yet we mark it
with our notch
day-by-day.
What we do
with our precious time
only you can say.

February 21, 1990

On Eagles Wings

I write
from the heart
from the dust
of my bin.
Yet in English 104
that's not
how it's been.

To research,
to gather
and collate
the facts.
Like nuts
to a squirrel
pondering their mass.

So I do
as I'm told
and chafe
at the bit.
Crying and clawing
that my spirit
may lift.

To let my
words fly
to go
where they will.
In company
with eagles,
no wax
on my wings.

March 6, 1990

MacArthur

Old Money I knew
Parson was home.
Now the Student Center
has an Egyptian Dome.
And 16 years later
I pick up the past.
Four kids and a divorce
some experience
has passed.

So what am I doing,
just clownin' around?
Rather retrieving
my dreams
from the lost
and the found.
So off I go,
just one class,
it's a breeze.
I can handle it all
have it all
with such ease.

'Til the dishes pile up,
the kids are sleeping over.
The laundry's not done,
it sure ain't clover.
I'm late for work
and Sue says
"Do I love her?"

Trying to remember,
where am I going?
Where was I last?
Waking up, rushing,
writing my works.
What time is it past?
Speeding down Plank Road
like a bat out of Hell.
Gosh darn it, I'm late
I'm late for Dowdell!

Slowly, I realize
that college must wait.
That I am but human,
not perfect, not great.
With a tinging of sadness
do I withdraw.
To come back strong,
robust in the fall.
And I will be back
And I 'will' be back
Again ...
and again.

March 8, 1990

25th Reunion Dream

Damaged   (lungs)
Broken   (leg)
Imprisoned (draft dodger)
Divorced &
Dislocated   (shoulder)

Breathing Free of the Wind
Not broken or bound
I remain One
With God and Family
Rooted in place
While Old Mountain waits.

August 9, 1992

Warm Embers

The Fire of Your Love
Pierces My Soul
It envelopes and engulfs
And burns me from within,
Empower and Impassion,
Not consuming in ashes.

These Two Bright Lights
Of Flames atwirlin'
A symbol for the dawn,
Gives One for Loving,
The Other to shine back upon
A mirror of our beauty.

Encircle, Intwine
Embrace, Intrance
Draw around close and hear,
While I offer you these love drops
And whisper
Merry Christmas, My Dear.

December 20, 1992

Christmas Gift

A man on a mission
Intent was I
On going Christmas shopping
Ere the stores say good-bye
And a husband be found lacking.

Of a present for my dearest
My dearest of dears
A little something for my love
Just something for her ears.

Walking in the shoppe
A quick peruse I did
No, that's not right
This won't do
I was getting in a snid.

Then some small voices rose
I barely could hear,
Them quite saying
"Over here, over here!"
Yes, there they were
The perfect pair
And a birthstone to match
It just seemed right fair.

So don't get cross
No don't get mad
It's only my way
Of saying I'm glad
That I am married
To You!

No money can't buy
A sum of one's love
No money can't buy
True kisses and hugs
Yes money is just a thing
To show one the way
That this is my present
For what you give every day
That I Love You.

December 24, 1994

Nebraska Passage

A Nebraska soldier boy
meets a Chicago city girl
on a summer train
in the plains.
A chance encounter
of steel and flint
produce sparks and love,
without a hint
of what will be,
as two lives
come together.

Of East and West
two different worlds,
one of manners
and one of basics,
the ways of refinement
vs the emotions of confinement
not to be wasted
when tears are too few
for sorrows a'many.

And the woman
pulled the man
away from his home.
For he wanted a union
a love to enclose
to seek and to find
the closure of his soul.
His other half
that was missing
the rib torn asunder.
He gave up his home.
He gave up his thunder.

For this was the American Way.
That a woman should lead
and the man would but follow.
Yet for a family foundation
when there's no male,
is but hollow.
And the walls do crumble
over time
as they say,
solid and joined
will last all our days;
and single and cracked
will fall down
in the mine of confusion.

It was a gulf of love
that brought them together.
Yet they could not cross
that stormy sea weather
of misunderstanding.
And viewed each other
from the other side
not knowing, still caring,
of how they could hide
out from each other.

And in their passing
they sewed their own quilt
of people and places
of children and love,
and myriad faces
that dot each square
with a story to tell.
One knows not the whole story
only what one can dwell
on the germs of the truth,
the brew of the past,
what portions we drink
what knowledge we fast
upon our brains lest they idle
of what has gone on before,
our previous histories
our once was no mores.

So I walk around
I carry this about
the push and the pull
the quiet and the shout.
Of the finest of things
and the rawest of earth.
Of what is my wont?
Of what is my birth?

That Chicago is the edge
of the East
and a tone
of hustle and bustle
of hard shells
not home.
That Nebraska is in
the middle of things
it's under a sky
that goes on and on
and sings and sings.
Where you can taste
the dirt on the wind
and look down for miles
on all of God's things.

That I am a product
of history and home,
I just open my channel
and the voices hone
a loud clear cry
that cries through my bones:
Of reaching
and touching,
To sing out and be still
To yearn and to learn
and yet be nil
Should I NOT say
To All
To me
To YOU
and to ONE
that you must
be your best
until the day
you are done.

December 31, 1994

Way

Pine Ridge Country Nebraska

Tonto Natural Bridge State Park Arizona

Out

Mogollon Mountains New Mexico

Indian Gardens Grand Canyon Arizona

West

Black Hills South Dakota

San Juan Mountains Colorado

O

St. Boniface Basilica Manitoba

Banff - Jasper Highway Alberta

Canada

Lake Louise Alberta

Kananaskis Alberta

Near

Black Hawk Statue Oregon, Illinois

Devils Lake State Park Wisconsin

To

White Pines State Park Illinois
Elizabeth, Sue, Tracy, Matt, Peter and Steven (hidden), Anna,
Emily, Jean, Will, Mary and Jim (clockwise from bottom)

Eagle Harbor Door County, Wisconsin

Home

Starved Rock State Park Illinois

Our home

Front Cover–Starved Rock Lodge Illinois
Back Cover–Author at Snowy Range Pass Wyoming

86

- Notes -

- Notes -

To order additional copies of **Mostly Me**, complete the information below.

Ship to: (please print)

Name _____

Address _____

City, State, Zip _____

Day phone _____

_____ copies of **Mostly Me** @ $8.00 each	$_____
Postage and handling is $2.00	$_____
Illinois residents add 6.5% tax	$_____
Total amount enclosed	$_____

*Make checks payable to **Buckingham Publications***

Send to: Buckingham Publications
P.O. Box 602 • Crystal Lake, IL 60039-0602

To order additional copies of **Mostly Me**, complete the information below.

Ship to: (please print)

Name _____

Address _____

City, State, Zip _____

Day phone _____

_____ copies of **Mostly Me** @ $8.00 each	$_____
Postage and handling is $2.00	$_____
Illinois residents add 6.5% tax	$_____
Total amount enclosed	$_____

*Make checks payable to **Buckingham Publications***

Send to: Buckingham Publications
P.O. Box 602 • Crystal Lake, IL 60039-0602